Spelling Disaster

A Spooky Cat Story

C.H. Lyn

Horizon Publishing

Contents

Content Warning

- Blood & Gore

One

There is something lovely about a Saturday morning farmers market. Even if I do have to hide Skia in my oversized hoodie the whole time. They aren't the best at picking out eggs, but they somehow always know which cantaloupe is ripe.

It's a beautiful start to the day. Until I catch sight of a leather vest, spiked blond hair, and a pair of aviator sunglasses.

My cantaloupe cracks on the concrete.

The day takes a decided turn.

• • • • • • • • • • •

"Run."

The instruction is unnecessary, but I heed Skia's frantic command and sprint down the side alley as fast as my legs can carry me—us. Skia is in the hood of my sweater, their favorite place to be and the only reason I'm wearing one when it's nearly ninety-three degrees outside.

A choice I regret as my arms pump at my sides, adrenaline replacing the fear in my blood.

Our farmers market treats are scattered across the sidewalk. A necessary sacrifice to maintain distance from the man pursuing us.

Footsteps pound the asphalt behind me: the heavy black boots of a man who looks like a mercenary straight out of an action movie as he gives chase.

A knife flies past me and thunks into the brick wall to my left. Too close.

"I told you," I huff, "not to… practice… outside of Agatha's."

"Is now the time?" Skia's voice in my head is more scared than I've heard it all summer.

We've been dodging Axel—a bounty hunter hired by hell—for over a month. The man caught our trail after Agatha used some harmless magic at a wedding ceremony. Turns out all magic is trackable, not just Skia's special brand of demonic power.

"Can't run forever," calls a distinct, winded Australian accent. I glance back and catch sight of the bounty hunter pulling another weapon from his belt.

I stuff my "I told you so" rant away for later and focus on the map in my head. I've lived in this city for years. I know these streets. The roads and alleys and shops that make up downtown are a maze for most.

For me, it's a jungle gym.

I zip left down a busy street, dart into a small corner store, and with a nod at the old Korean woman behind the counter, hurry through the building and out into a new alley. Then I double back the way we just came from, slowing at intersections to make sure Axel isn't waiting.

"Lost him," Skia breathes, their voice just a whisper across the front of my mind.

I nod. "Get into the front pocket."

They obey. A shadow of black glides across my shoulder and down into the front pocket of my hoodie. I push the sleeves up past my elbows, breathing hard and making a mental note to never forget Skia's travel backpack again. It's hot.

I do another quick check to make sure a towering, black-leather clad man with multiple rune-inscribed knives and trinkets hasn't found us. Pretty sure we left him in the dust several blocks back, but few things would be worse than accidentally leading Axel to Agatha's Emporium.

After ensuring Skia has no whisps of smoke sticking out of my pockets—both for appearances and because they would burn away in the sun—I step onto a main thoroughfare full of people and begin an as-neutral-as-possible stroll to my friend's shop.

• • • • ● • ● • • •

"Why do you insist on participating in classes full of falsehoods?"

I sigh and close my laptop. Free of the hoodie and enjoying the air-conditioned comfort of Agatha's Emporium, I'm a bit more relaxed.

There is also the plus of having warding sigils all over the place here. Nothing strong enough to attract attention, but according to Agatha and Skia the runes keep us somewhat invisible and allow Skia to use their own personal store of power without alerting Axel's tracking capabilities.

They mute the "disturbance of magical energy." Whatever that means.

"I want to know how different places and peoples think of stuff like this." I gesture vaguely at Skia—sitting in the right bowl of an antique scale, Agatha—behind the counter measuring ingredients into little containers, and Missy—cocking her head at me with an appraising look I still haven't gotten used to.

"Why? Humans know nothing."

"Hey," Agatha barks from her stool behind the counter. She gives Skia a squinty glare, her sparkling purple eyelids nearly closing. Her eyeliner is needle-sharp, hair pinned back in a messy bun while she works, and lips as vibrant red as ever.

Skia adjusts their words. *"Next to nothing."*

Ags rolls her eyes, but her temper cools as Missy hops onto the countertop for pets.

I grin. My little black cat has been making a habit of emerging for snuggles whenever the late summer heat gets on any of our nerves. Or when a bounty hunter nearly catches us on accident because we wandered through the farmers market at the wrong time.

"The point isn't to take everything in these classes as gospel," I say with an exhale. I stretch and crack my neck. My shirt is still damp from sweat. "But if we want to travel, find more people with abilities like Ags, and learn more about what is going on with all this magic stuff, it'd be good to have an idea of what people already think."

Agatha nods, then looks to the front door. It's a Saturday, but summer has been slow for business. Things will likely pick up when autumn falls in.

"When do classes start?" she asks.

I grimace. "I can sign up in a week, then actual classes are another month out. But I'm thinking I should go back to all online."

A furrow mars her smooth bronze skin. "Why?"

It's my turn to glance toward the front of the shop. A sinking feeling makes my stomach clench.

The spring wedding Agatha officiated was beautiful. But the preceding danger to Skia, and the proceeding fear of being chased by a bounty hunter working for *hell*, was and is a lot on the nerves. I haven't gotten a good night of sleep since we left the east coast.

"Axel isn't going to stop hunting us," I murmur, not wanting to drop the mood. "Going to classes at the same time on consistent days of the week feels kinda dumb. He doesn't know what you look like." I give Ags a nod. "But my face is recognizable."

Even after the haircut, Skia agrees. Their little shadowy self bounces just enough to shift the scales.

At the counter, Missy mews. Ags scratches behind her ear with long nails.

"We'll figure something—" Agatha begins. But she's cut off by a little jingle from the front door.

Missy leaps from the counter, hurrying to the cushy armchair next to mine and pawing at the pillow. Skia darts to it, their shape conforming to the shadowy space made available. Missy curls up beside it.

From more than a foot away it looks as though Skia is simply my cat's shadow.

I stand, worry caught in my throat even as I marvel at how ridiculously smart Missy has become.

The quickening of my pulse is steadied as Agatha's lips split into a smile.

"Welcome to Agatha's Emporium," she calls, striding around the counter and making toward the young blonde woman who has just entered the shop. "What can I do for you today?"

I follow Ags at a casual pace, curious about the hurried look of the woman who just pushed through the doors.

She appears to be in her early twenties with a high pony and wide green eyes. Both hands are in front of her chest, clutching something small in her fingers. She takes a deep breath.

"I need your help."

Two

"Start at the beginning."

I glance at Ags, then cross to the chair where Skia is still hiding behind the shadow of a pillow and perch on the edge. Missy rises and gracefully leaps to the floor.

Across from me, the blonde woman, Kate, sits straight-backed and tense on a footstool. Offers for her to take the remaining comfy chair were met with vehement head shaking.

Her hair is long, flowy and curled with a gentle wave at the end of the ponytail. Her cheeks are still flushed, either from the heat outside or the hurry to get here. An old Jan Sport backpack dangles from her shoulder. She hasn't made any move to put it down.

Curiosity threatens to shoo away my manners because her hands are still tight to her chest, but I'm pretty sure I just saw something move between her fingers.

A whisper of suspicion stirs in my veins. A warning to remain alert around this woman. There was a time I'd ignore my instincts, call them paranoia, but not after everything my little family has been through these past few months.

"Easy." Skia's murmurs in my head. *"You're practically squishing me. Relax."*

I shift to the side, wishing I was able to respond in the same way. But speaking directly into people's heads is a demonic trait that cannot be learned.

They're right though. I'm on edge. I rest my hand on the cushion and a thin tendril of smoke curls around my pinky in a comforting gesture.

Agatha settles into the vacant chair, crossing her hands delicately over in her lap and giving Kate a look that reminds me of every fortune-teller I've ever seen in a movie. Even her skirts are splayed out in a way that oozes mysticism.

Kate glances my way for a fraction of a second. I give a tight smile.

"It's all right." Ags' soothing voice seems to bring calm to the trembling woman. "This is a safe place. Tell us what happened."

Missy rubs against my shin, and I reach down to give her a pet. She sniffs the air.

"So, it was right after the semester ended." Kate speaks with urgency. She looks at Ags as she stumbles over her story. "My best friend got dumped, so she borrowed a book from my Nona and then came here wanting to get stuff for, like, a witchy girl's night or whatever. She got herbs and some chalk and candles and stuff."

Agatha nods.

I ignore the silent scoff that echoes in my head and adjust the pillow Skia is hiding behind.

Missy pads toward our guest, her little black nose in the air as though she's caught the scent of bacon.

"Well, they ended up getting back together so that didn't happen." Kate's strained expression slips into an angry frown. "But last week I found out Trevor was cheating on me with *two different girls* from our sociology class, and then when I confronted him, he said it was my fault for prioritizing school work over our relationship."

I grimace. Ags murmurs her condolences. Kate grits her teeth for a second, then shakes her head and sucks in a deep breath.

"Anyway, we had all the stuff from here, and the book, and three bottles of wine from a wedding we just went to and... It was supposed to just be for fun. I don't even believe in any of that junk. But then..." Her eyebrows draw together in a look of such desperation that a flash of pity surges through me. "It was an accident. And I don't know how to fix it..."

Missy turns her yellow eyes on me for a brief second, her whiskers twitching with mischief. She prances closer to Kate, tilting her head as she sniffs the woman's hands.

Kate lets out half a broken chuckle and smiles down at the cat.

Keeping her fingers together like a cage, Kate reveals what she's been holding onto this whole time. A small green and white lizard blinks out from between her palms.

Its tongue flicks out, licking its eyeball before it catches sight of Missy and begins scurrying frantically back and forth in Kate's hands.

I raise an eyebrow, confusion slowly melting into horror as, in my head, Skia says, *"Oh my."*

Kate inhales, looking from me to Agatha with her brows pinched together in a desperate frown. "This is my ex."

Three

We barely have time to process when the lizard—Trevor—slips through Kate's fingers and shoots across the floor like a kid on a slip-and-slide.

"Missy, no!" I jump after the cat, but she's given chase.

The lizard scurries under a hutch displaying an assortment of crystal balls. Missy barrels toward it with all the intent of a predator cornering her prey.

"Do *not* break Agatha's things," I snap.

That seems to do it. Missy backpedals into a stop only an inch from the ornate wooden shelving unit. She narrows her yellow eyes at me and bares her teeth.

I sigh. "That's not a normal lizard, Missy. You can't chase it around."

She flicks her tail.

"Or eat it," I mutter as I get on all fours and duck my head to try and find the damn thing.

Sure enough, the green and white man-turned-reptile is cowering in the least accessible corner. I reach, but it scootches back even further. My shoulder can't get under the hutch.

I retreat, scoop Missy into my arms, and join Agatha and Kate at the check-out counter where my friend is trying to calm the newcomer.

"Let's start simple," Ags says. Only knowing her for years allows me to detect the tension in her steady voice. "Do you have this book you mentioned?"

Kate nods, her eyes red from rubbing away tears. With her hands now free, she takes off her backpack, unzips it, and dumps the contents onto the counter.

A half-burned candle, twigs of some kind of herb, a sandwich baggie of ash, and a thick book that looks older than the Presidency all pour out.

"This is everything," Kate says with a glance at the hutch. "Should we... do you have anything we can put him in while we talk?"

I give Missy ear scratches to try and pacify her. The usual purrs are replaced with a glowering look at me. I roll my eyes and turn my attention to Kate.

"Took a while to catch him the first time?"

"Yeah," she says with a grimace. "It's why I didn't get here right when you opened. I spent most of the morning trying to find him in my apartment."

Agatha meets my eye. "I think we know someone who could get him out of there." She digs around behind the counter and comes up with an old shoebox. "And I can poke some holes in this."

I huff out a breath. The past months have been spent keeping Skia hidden and safe. It feels abnormal to let a stranger see them.

Then again, this specific stranger turned her ex into a lizard last night. She's already in this weird world of magic. Whether she wants to be or not.

"I've got it," Skia hisses.

Kate jolts, backing against the counter as her wide eyes search for the source of the voice that just echoed through her head. "Who... what—"

"So, this is Skia," I say in as soothing a voice as possible.

My shadowy friend slinks out from under the pillow and drifts to the ground. They move like a cloud on the wind, only faster. It's a bit unsettling to see the first few times, and I step in front of Kate so she doesn't feel like they're coming right at her.

"What..." She swallows and takes a deep breath before continuing. "What is it, exactly?"

Skia slides toward the hutch, glinting red eyes the only way to tell where their front is.

"They're a sneeze demon." I turn to her. "And they'll probably be able to get Trevor out from under the hutch."

"Right." Kate's voice is soft and high. After a few seconds of bewildered blinking, she straightens and turns to Agatha. "Do you think you can turn him back into an asshole?"

I snort.

Skia's haunting laugh dances through everyone's heads again.

Kate blanches but keeps her eyes on Agatha.

My friend gives a faltering smile. "I can look at all of this, but I don't want to promise anything. I've never—" She glances at me.

I move closer, setting Missy on the counter and looking at Kate. "Ags does defensive magic. All protection-type stuff. And even with that, we're still new to actual, practical magic."

Kate lets out a shaky exhale. "But you sell all of this."

I give a weak shrug. "Yeah, for people who want to practice wiccan stuff. For those wine and witchy nights."

"It's only recently that my magic has begun working in a more real sense," Ags murmurs. "But we've not... you're the first person who has come in like this."

Kate gestures vaguely around the shop. "But... none of it is supposed to be real, I—"

I cut her off as gently as possible. "This is new to us all."

Agatha and I exchange a brief look.

I continue, "Can you tell us exactly what you did?"

There is a pause in the conversation as Skia swoops out from under the hutch. The lizard is caught in a makeshift cage created with whisps of their smoke-like substance.

"Where is the creature's prison?"

Ags fights back a smile and takes off the lid to the shoe box. Skia deposits the lizard, and she quickly puts the lid back in place. Just before a little black paw darts towards it.

"Missy," Ags scolds.

The cat lets out a defeated yowl and slumps down onto the counter, her gaze trained onto the gray box.

Kate clears her throat and nods. "Right. So we found a page that looked good, drew some symbols on a sheet over the hardwood, and then drank a ton of wine and burned some candles. Then we watched Practical Magic, drank even more wine, and went to bed." She looks at her hands, desperate disbelief etched into her expression. "It wasn't supposed to actually *do* anything."

"How do you know that," I point at the box, "is Trevor?"

She rubs her temple. "He came over this morning to pick up some of his stuff and when he stepped on the sheet—"

"He melted into a reptile."

As pale as she is, it's hard to tell if Kate is still affected by Skia's voice or if she's already used to it.

She nods again. "He was screaming, I was screaming, and then there was a freaking lizard scurrying around my apartment. None of my friends believed me that it's Trevor, but I watched it happen."

"A delay on the spell." Skia's voice carries a thoughtful tone. *"That suggests powerful magic."*

Kate swallows. With a nervous glance at the demon, she looks at Agatha. "Can you help me?"

Ags looks at me, her eyes wide with uncertainty. "I'm still not sure how you managed..."

The hesitation in her voice sends a pang of sadness through me. My friend likes having the answers. She likes knowing things and sharing that knowledge with others. Finding herself unable to help someone has to hurt.

I brush my fingers across the array of things Kate dumped on the counter. As I reach the book, Skia speaks again.

"You didn't get this here." They follow my movements, gliding over to the book in question and appraising it with glowing red eyes.

"No," Kate says. "It's my Nona's."

"This has... far too much magic."

Worry stirs in my stomach at the tension in Skia's voice.

"Too much for the wards?" Ags asks. She reaches for her oversized purse.

"It's very possible."

Agatha nods, exchanges a glance with me, and begins shoveling items into her bag.

I look at Kate. "Where *is* your Nona? We might need to go pay a visit."

Four

Getting to Kate's Nona's house sounds like it will be simple enough. She lives a couple of hours outside the city on a nonoperational ranch their family used to run. All we have to do is get to Agatha's car—a little junker she keeps parked in the multi-level garage on the corner–and make our way east.

Sounds simple.

Until Skia, perched on my shoulder as I pack up my things, says something that sinks a stone-like weight into my gut.

"Agatha, is the front door locked?"

We all turn as one.

Kate glances from the door to the rest of us, her eyes wide. "Do you guys know that dude?"

Standing on the other side of the tinted glass is Axel. His face is slightly obscured by the shelves between us and the window, but there is no mistaking the black pants, leather vest, and multitude of weapons on his belt. He moves slowly, taking in the storefronts.

"I did lock it, Skia," Agatha murmurs. She does up the last buckle on her purse and pats her shoulder.

Missy leaps from the counter to the patted spot in a graceful movement.

"But I don't imagine that will hold him for long." Ags hefts her purse and strides purposefully toward the back of the shop.

Kate looks at me and Skia. "So you *do* know that guy."

"It's a long story," Skia says. *"I'll happily explain... once we're well away from him."*

Kate raises an eyebrow, her gaze sliding from Skia's red eyes to my hazel ones.

I nod. "We really should go."

She snatches her backpack from the chair and hurries after me. We follow Agatha past the checkout counter, through a sparkly black curtain, and down a long narrow hallway.

I pull open the heavy exterior door that leads to the parking garage access walkway. Kate hurries through and, as I turn to follow her, the crash of breaking glass sounds behind me.

• • • ● • ● ● • •

"Faster," Skia urges. Their voice is not in my head alone, evidenced by Kate's shift from walking to jogging.

Further ahead, Missy has opted to run alongside Agatha rather than ride her shoulder in the rush to escape.

"Who the hell is that guy?" Kate demands, glancing back at me.

"Who the hell indeed."

Even with fear gripping me tight, I can't help a half-hearted chuckle.

"Bounty hunter," I say.

I catch up to her, jogging alongside as we take a sharp right and are spat out into a large parking garage. Shadows loom behind every column. Parked cars are both places to hide and places people—or demons—might be lurking.

"Bounty hunter?" Kate's incredulous tone echoes against the concrete walls and ceiling.

"Shh."

I take a left, following Agatha's flowing skirts as she swishes rapidly through the cars to her beat-up, tan Toyota Corolla.

"Yep," I say in a hushed voice as Agatha unlocks the car and we all pile in. "A bounty hunter. Hired by hell. There's an essence or aura or something that goes off when people use magic. From what we can tell, this guy has been tracking down those auras."

Ags turns the key, throws the Corolla in reverse, and pulls out of the parking spot.

Kate twists in the passenger seat, starting at me with a horrified expression. "What does he do when he finds them?"

"Great question." I take off my backpack and set it on the floor, then lean across the backseat to lock the door. "To be honest, we haven't been that keen to find out."

Skia lets out a laugh lightly tinged with fear. Then they stop. They shift on the seat and for a moment I think they're worried about the sunlight about to stream through the windows. I get my sweater ready for them to hide under but...

"Demi."

Then I also realize what's missing.

"Wait!" I curse under my breath, leaning forward to glance at the front with little hope that I'll find what I'm looking for.

Both women look back at me, bewildered.

I slap a hand to my forehead.

"We forgot the damn lizard."

Five

This seems unwise.

I nod; Skia is correct. This is unwise.

Unwise, but necessary. Because we have no clue what happens to magical stuff when Axel gets ahold of it, and as much of a jerk as Trevor sounds like, I don't think we should test the limits of hell's cruelty on the guy.

So, with Skia tucked into the large pocket of my sweatshirt—again—I press against the exterior front wall of Agatha's Emporium, preparing myself to run in and grab the shoebox containing a cheating ex-boyfriend.

Ags, Missy, and Kate wait in the car just around the corner. An SOS is all set in the message app on my phone, resting beside Skia in my pocket. The car is in drive, ready to race down the alley as soon as Skia's shadow tendrils push send.

But first we have to get the box.

I scoot along the side, my hood snagging on the bricks as I approach the shattered front door.

I cringe at the thought of Agatha having to pay for all of this. Glass is strewn across the pavement, and it doesn't sound as though Axel is being particularly careful with Agatha's delicate items.

"He sounds like an elephant in a tea shop."

I push past the desire to correct my demon friend and step carefully through the jagged threshold.

Axel is somewhere near the back of the store, based on where all the noise is coming from.

Glass crunches under my shoes, but the sound is minimal compared to the clanging and cursing.

"Careful." Skia's shadow head pokes out of my pocket.

I can't respond, but I have to believe the thundering of my pulse is audible to their demon senses. Of course I'm being careful.

I move through the shop quickly. The shelves help block me from view, but they also stop me from seeing exactly where Axel is. I step around the final obstacle and spot the shoebox. It sits in the center of the check-out counter.

Fully in the open.

Down the dark hall, the banging stops.

I grit my teeth, dart forward, and snatch the box.

"Well, well, well, look who finally showed themselves."

My breath catches, heart pounding as a massive hand—clad in a fingerless glove with little studs on the knuckles—pushes aside Agatha's sparkly curtain and a very large man steps into the main room of the store.

Axel's thick Australian drawl and his spiked dirty-blond hair threaten to be mildly humorous, but the multitude of daggers at his belt and the glinting, predatory look in his eye solidify the instinct to be afraid.

"Just picking up something. Feel free to continue the wreckage." I gesture at the shards of broken glass, shredded pieces of paper, and scatterings of dirt from many destroyed plants, without taking my eyes off the bounty hunter.

"You've been evading me for a while now." He steps forward, boots crunching the glass, gaze scanning me in a way that feels more like an airport x-ray than the usual creepy-guy eyeing. "Ahh," he says as he catches sight of my large hoodie pocket, "that's where you're hiding."

"*Less hiding,*" Skia says in both our heads. "*More catching a ride.*"

In my own head, they continue, "*Demi, move slowly. Back us toward the door.*"

I obey. Axel follows. His boots are loud on the ground, but a soft jingle also catches my attention. A small silver trinket hangs from a leather cord attached to his belt.

"Don't try anything stupid here, kid."

My lips twist in a grimace. "What exactly do you want with us?"

"*Keep going.*"

I take another few steps, slowly moving backward while I keep my eyes on Axel. This face to face has been coming for a while now. My grip is so tight I'm making little divots in the shoebox.

"*Don't let him get too close.*" Skia whispers through my head again.

"I wasn't planning to," I growl.

Axel, mouth open and about to answer my question, cocks his head. "Ahh. The two of you are having a private conversation? That's rude."

"Rude?" My incredulity momentarily steals my common sense. "Rude is tracking people across the country and destroying their livelihood."

A brief flush reddens the bounty hunter's cheeks as he glances around the store.

"Rude is snatching up magical things and doing who-knows-what with them."

"Accepting a bounty from hell might be considered rude."

Axel snarls. "Stay outta my head, demon."

I step backward again. The busted door to the shop is only about ten feet from me now. The summer heat presses against my sweatshirt, fighting the air conditioning of Agatha's store.

"That *thing* doesn't belong here." Axel's hand moves to his side.

I swallow as he pulls a silver blade from its sheath and points the tip at my chest.

"Why not?" I demand. If I keep him talking maybe I can get through the door before he lunges. Then again, maybe I'll end up with a dagger in my back.

"It's unnatural," Axel's voice, the words themselves, grate against my nerves.

I shake my head and take another half step. All that's left between us and freedom is a rickety bookshelf that once held flower vases and candles. It's empty now, the shelves themselves barely more than splintered wood.

"What is? A demon?"

"All of it." He flips the blade in his hand. "The demon, the magic, you helping it... it's upsetting the balance. Which is why you gotta go, and that demon has to come with me."

"I'm hitting the button," Skia says to me. *"Keep him talking. Find out what they're paying him."*

"Why you?" I ask, unable to respond to Skia with anything besides pressing the box tighter to my chest. "Why didn't hell just keep sending demons?"

"And put even more of them on our plane?" He scoffs. "You don't get it. Any of it. What else would I expect from some Yank with no training in the mystic."

Despite the absolute truth of his words, I'm offended.

"Why are you stopping?" Skia's tone is a mix of frightened and annoyed.

I skip over my frustration. "What is hell giving you to make it worth all this effort?"

Axel sneers. He flips the blade again, shifting his stance as though he's about to pounce.

"Your weight in gold, kid. Any last words?"

I hear something in the distance. The squeal of tires. The gurgle of a very old Toyota Corolla engine.

"Yeah." I heave a sigh and shake my head. "You're ruining Steve Irwin's accent for me."

I side-step and, with a grunt of effort, shove the bookshelf. Already off kilter from Axel's earlier rampage, it goes down hard and fast. Right on top of the man.

Skia and I are gone before he manages to scramble to his feet.

I leap through the open door to Agatha's backseat, nearly colliding with Kate, and Ag's peels out of the alley.

Six

The route to Kate's Nona's house is fraught with tension. Partially because all three of the humans keep glancing back to check if Axel is tailing us—we have no idea what he drives, but I can only assume it's a very loud motorcycle. Partially because Skia has taken on a sulky demeanor and refuses to tell me why—even only in my head. And partially because Missy—as intelligent as she is after everything we've been through—has not ceased her efforts to capture and, I assume, eat the lizard.

Leaving the city doesn't take too long despite the usual Saturday afternoon traffic. We hit the plains, and Agatha follows Kate's directions down various backroads until the sun is low. The sepia-toned skyline seems flat despite the mountain range not far to the west.

Kate instructs Agatha to turn, and I swallow audibly.

"Uh, is this the place?"

Skia glides up from where they were resting on the floor of the car. They nestle into my lap, no longer in danger of the sun.

"Hmm. Spooky."

I nod as Kate chuckles.

"Yeah. This is the family ranch. It used to be operational, but my dad left when he joined the army, and the rest of the aunts and uncles didn't have an interest in running things. So, it's just Nona now."

We pass under a large arched sign with missing letters. I'm unsure what it once said, but at present it reads *Cail--ach Ranc-*.

Ivy crawls up the wrought iron. Spiderwebs shimmer in the dim evening light. The gravel road leads through what appears to be waist-high fields of golden grass. Ahead, a three-story ranch house sits not far from an almost-as-large fading red barn. The only height around us comes from the buildings and a few scraggly trees surrounding them.

The lack of mountains, forests, anything on the horizon sends a shiver down my spine.

"This place has a... peculiar feel to it," Agatha murmurs. She drives slowly, taking us up to the house.

"There is strong magic here."

Kate glances into the backseat with alarm in her gaze. She meets Skia's eye and quickly turns back around.

Missy darts to my side, probably sensing my anxiety. I run my fingers through her fur, and her warmth calms me.

The car slows to a stop. Only one downstairs window of the house is lit. The rest are black, gaping holes of darkness that, when combined with the peeling paint and dripping gutters, seem as though they want to swallow us whole.

I pull my sweatshirt back on, grateful to have it as I creak open the door and step into chilly evening air. The city holds a different kind of heat and, though I'm certain temperatures were high during the day, the disappearance of the sun leaves an unseasonable cold in the air.

Or maybe I'm shivering because I'm freaked out.

"How is this place," I mutter just for Skia's ears, "creepier than a coven of witches opening a pit to hell?"

They let out a light hissing laugh and reply, *"Because you watch too many horror movies."*

Agatha gracefully steps out from the driver's seat, her multitude of skirts flowing behind her as the wind catches her hair.

"How do you look good after driving for two hours?" I grumble. I rub my face, dragging lines of sleep from my features as Skia takes their place at my shoulder.

Agatha lets out a soft chuckle. She looks around, eyes wide as she takes in the homestead-style house and barn. There are a multitude of garden beds between both. Raised boxes overflow with greenery. Chicken-wire surrounds many of them, a barricade to keep whatever animals live out here from stealing vegetables.

Ags gives her skirts a flourish and runs a hand through her hair. "Magic."

I roll my eyes, hearing the joke in her voice even as I push away a taste of bitterness.

"Wait, Missy!" Ags calls as the little black cat scampers past.

"It's okay," I say with humor in my voice.

Missy leaps, bounding through the tall grass like a dancer. Her little yowls are happy ones and, after a minute of sprinting and spinning halfway across the field and back, she returns to my side and rubs against my shin.

I kneel on one knee. "Nice change of pace?"

Those yellow eyes fix on me. She flicks her tail across my hand.

"After this, I'll make a point of taking you to the park more."

Missy meows.

"I'll be sure to remind them," Skia promises.

With a darted glance at the demon on my shoulder, my cat rubs her head across my hand. I give the ear scratches she's asking for and then rise to my feet.

Kate stands a few paces closer to the house, clutching the shoebox in her hands and looking back at us expectantly.

"Right, coming," I say.

"Do we want to hide the car or anything?" Agatha asks. "In case Axel catches up?"

I glance at the junker and then at the long drive we came up. "I think if he gets here, it's because he knows where we are. Feels like hiding the car won't do much."

Ags nods, clicks the lock on her key fob, and follows me toward the house.

We make it up the rickety steps of the wrap around porch. A wide swing sits to the left, looking as though it has had better days and squeaking as a gentle breeze causes it to sway.

"Not getting less creepy," I murmur to Skia on my shoulder.

The demon hisses a laugh again.

Kate crooks an eyebrow up at me. She shifts the shoebox under one arm and reaches up to knock on the white, paint peeling door.

Before her knuckles find the wood, a shadow moves across the glass pane square, the handle turns, and the door swings open.

• • • • • • • • • •

Nona is old. Old beyond what I'd expected from a grandmother of a twenty-something-year-old.

Her hunched figure screams crone, gnarled knuckle bones protrude at odd angles, and liver spots are barely visible against the multitude of freckles and wrinkles coating her skin. Her hair is white, each strand thick and coarse. She wears it long, braided nearly to her waist and decorated with wooden beads and dried out flowers.

Her stern expression breaks into a grin the second Kate's face is illuminated by the foyer light.

With ushering hands and a gravely voice, she pulls us all into the house.

"Nona." Kate deposits the shoebox onto a long end table and clutches her grandmother, burying her face in the woman's neck. She's nearly bent in half to collect the comfort from the much shorter woman.

"Katelyn," Nona says, patting her back. "My dear girl."

I swallow down a lump in my throat. Beside me, Agatha reaches out. Her hand closes around mine and she gives me a squeeze. Missy presses against my legs. A whisp of Skia's shadowy form caresses my neck.

Their presence lightens some of the weight settled against my chest.

I grew up in a place similar to this. Open fields, wide farmlands. Small towns and small minds. I had one ally growing up. My grandmother.

Her passing was what sparked me to get out of that place.

I blink away the tears burning in my eyes and try to focus on the décor. A set of stairs to the right is walled with family pictures. More dried plants, in vases and hanging from just about every place a hook would fit. And, as I carefully look everywhere but at the hug, I note things that I'd have missed a year ago.

There are scratches on the baseboards. Vaguely familiar symbols. I glance up and, sure enough, there are similar designs carved into the doorframe and the window ledges.

"Tell me, Kate," Nona's gravely voice grabs my attention. The woman gives us a cursory look; her eyes linger on Skia with a suspicious lack of surprise or fear. She turns to the box in Kate's hands. "What did the poor man do to deserve scales?"

Seven

Kate tells the story. From the infidelity to the purchasing of goods at Agatha's Emporium. When Nona raises an eyebrow, she sheepishly admits to her friend "borrowing" a "witchy-looking" book from Nona's library the last time they came for a visit.

To my surprise, the old woman doesn't look angry in the slightest. Instead, she cackles and tells Kate she's always liked that friend of hers.

We sit around a wooden kitchen table. Herbs dangle from every inch of wall space, much of which is taken by warped wooden shelves stacked with everything from cookbooks to unnamed tombs that look as old as the one Kate showed us, glass jars with an assortment of odd things in them—and some more recognizable like salt, pepper, and cinnamon. The kitchen also includes a wall of hanging pots and pans, as well as one of those magnetic knife holders with a row of sharp instruments.

In the center of the table, a little gray shoebox holds the green and white lizard.

Introductions are made. Nona's lack of curiosity at Skia is explained when she politely asks them which brand of demon they are.

I hear the surprise in their voice as they whisper the answer across our minds. I'm certain we both share a curiosity about how this woman knows so much, but the question is cut off before it begins when Nona looks at Agatha and raises an eyebrow.

"I'm wondering why you lot came all this way when you could have handled this yourself."

"Oh." Ags glances at me, her dark eyes wide. "Well, I'm actually pretty new to this. I've done wiccan ceremonies for years, but actual magic is—"

"New to this plane, yes. I know dear. But it sounds like you're well read, and you had the book." She puts a hand on the top of the leatherbound tomb. "I'm glad you've all brought it back, but it does surprise me."

"There was more than one reason for coming here," Skia says. They sit on the table in front of me, enjoying a plate of gingersnap cookies while Missy looks on from Ag's lap with a jealous gaze. *"But this feels more like witch magic than the wiccan craft."*

Ags nods.

Nona scoffs. "What on earth are you talking about, my little demon friend?"

I clear my throat. "We ran across a coven of witches on the east coast not too long ago. I think it's the similarity of aggressive magic that feels like this isn't wiccan in nature."

"*Wiccan in nature*?" Nona's tone is heavy with incredulity. She throws a hand in the air, shaking her head and directing a glare at Ags and then Skia. "What nonsense."

"As we said," I mutter with growing annoyance. "We're brand new to all of this. Even Skia had been gone from this plane for over five-hundred years before they showed up in Missy."

"Yes." Nona turns her glare on me. "Showed up and reawakened a magic in the world that has been dormant for centuries."

Kate gulps.

Agatha shifts uncomfortably in her chair.

I glare back at the old woman.

Nona sighs. "It's not your fault," she placates, patting Ag's arm. "It sounds as though the two of you," she glanced from Ag's to Skia, "are of the belief that wiccan and witch mean two different things."

"Don't they?" I ask, my brow furrowed.

The shoebox at the center of the table wiggles. Missy's gaze shifts from the cookies to it, her eyes narrowed.

"Not in the slightest."

Agatha frowns. "I was always told wiccans work for the common good while witches aim for power, usually from demonic sources. The witches in Salem certainly seemed as though they felt the same."

"Young ones," Nona grumbles. "I'm plenty powerful without help from those bums in hell, thank you very much."

Her tone replaces my defensive frustration with a snort.

She grins at me. "Looks like we need a refill on cookies. And I could certainly use some tea if I'm going to spend my evening educating the lot of you and reversing my granddaughters ill-advised revenge spell."

Across the table, Kate flushes. She mumbles, "Sorry Nona."

"Oh, it's fine Katelyn. Now, put some water on to boil while I find the rest of the gingersnaps. Then the lesson begins."

"There is no true difference between wiccan magic and witchcraft. The terminology began to change when people who focused on healing and defensive magic were called wiccan by the populace. Those of us more geared toward offensive spells were deemed witches. There was plenty of cross casting, but of course, as with all things, rumors spread and politics came into it. After a few centuries, witches were painted in a much darker color than our wiccan counterparts. Though, as I said before, there is no true difference between the two."

Agatha stares open-mouthed at Nona. Awkward uncertainty clouds her expression as she swallows and begins an apology.

The grandmother—the witch—waves it away and takes a sip of her jasmine tea. "Worry over it no longer, darling. How could you possibly know? Rumors and gossip become truth when there is no one to teach real history."

I chuckle. "Who taught you the real history?"

"Took the question right outta my mouth," Kate says with a smirk. "And why didn't I know about any of this, Nona?"

Nona turns a glare on her granddaughter again. "Don't start with that. I've invited you over time and again to learn my old secrets, and you've reject every offer."

Kate doesn't flinch away from the tone, instead she rolls her eyes. "Well, I thought you were talking about farming secrets!"

Skia's haunting laugh fills the heads of everyone in the kitchen, and the rest of us join them in a round of chuckles.

Nona stands with a groan and pats Agatha's shoulder. "Don't worry yourself about it. I'm happy to share what I know with the new generation. Now." She surveys us as she fills her teacup again. "What is the other reason you came here?"

The last of my laughter dies in my throat. My expression sours as I recall the predatory look Axel trained on Skia back at Agatha's Emporium. Nona turns to me.

"Ohh," she murmurs. "Something serious then." She gestures a liver-spotted hand at the box on the table. "More serious than questionable spell-work."

Kate has the gall to look offended before she gives a half-hearted shrug and picks up a cookie.

"Our incident back east seems to have put us on the radar of a bounty hunter," Agatha says softly. "He's after Skia, though it seems he's also stealing anything magical he can find along the way."

Nona looks at Skia. "Who hired him?"

My lip curls. "Hell. According to what he said the first time he found us." I wave a hand agitatedly through the air. "There was a whole monologue."

"They do enjoy those," Nona says, her gaze still thoughtfully fixed on Skia. "And you don't want to go back?"

I move my hands, reaching across the table to curl my arms around my friend. "No, they don't."

"I'd rather not descend to the plane of fire and suffering again. No."

"And you all." Nona looks to the rest of us, taking her time to meet every eye. "You have no issue keeping a demon in your midst? You do not agree that this creature should be returned to damnation?"

Silence permeates the kitchen. My heartbeat thunders in my chest, a renewed worry for my friend seeping into my chest.

My jaw is tight as I stand from the table. The chair scrapes across the ground. "Skia has every right to exist," I murmur. "They have a right to be safe and happy and cared for."

"Demi."

The whisper of the word, in all our heads evidenced by the softening of Nona's expression.

Agatha nods.

Kate gives an audible gulp and then pipes up, "I haven't known Skia long, but they seem nice. And they didn't judge me for turning Trevor into a lizard so..."

"I wouldn't dare to judge you for the act. Even the spell itself was quite impressive, especially for one brand new to witchy magic."

"Brand new to magic," Agatha corrected softly. She frowned at the grandmother, who had picked up a bell jar and was sprinkling herbs into it. "Does this mean I can do more? More than the protection symbols and wards and things."

"Oh," Nona says with a grin. She turns, her face catching the light and giving her wrinkly skin an eeric glow. "Much more, deary. And I can help teach—"

Her offer is cut off by a sound that sends a shiver down my spine and causes my lower back to start sweating.

The distant roar of a motorcycle coming up the gravel path.

Eight

"Now is a good time to show our new friend the protection magic you've been practicing."

Skia darts across the table, hops over Kate's shoulder, and swishes up to look out the window above the sink. Plants cover the ledge, and Skia could almost be mistaken for a shadow amongst the multitude of dark leaves.

I move with them, leaning in toward the glass in time to catch sight of a headlight before it disappears behind the car. A second later, my guess that it's Axel is confirmed via the outline of the man against the moonlight as he strides toward the house.

Agatha sets Missy on the table and glances at Nona. "With your permission?"

Nona smiles, the curve of her lips brings her laugh lines into stark contrast. "This man has been following you for some time?"

I turn from the window and nod. "Seems like he's been look-ing for us for months."

The old woman sets down the bell jar. She pats Agatha's arm with a very grandmotherly smile. "Why don't you let me help with this one, dear. It's been a long while since I've had the opportunity to stretch my magic."

Missy yowls. Standing on the table she paws the lizard box once before jumping down. With a flick of her yellow eyes in my direction, she gestures with a paw and follows Nona and Agatha toward the front door.

Kate scoops the shoebox from the table, opens a cupboard, and tucks it inside. She glances at me. "Are you bringing any-thing to this fight with a bounty hunter from hell?"

I can't help but chuckle at her dry tone. Part of me takes offense to the question, but I push that part down. It's obvious she didn't mean anything by it. And it's a fair ask.

Still, magic or not I *need* a way to help my friends. So, I grab one of the knives on the magnet block and gesture her to lead the way.

Kate grins. "This is nuts." She takes a blade as well and hurries after the others.

"*Demi.*" Skia floats along the counter toward me, stopping a few inches from the point of the knife. "*I think you should stay in here.*"

I snort. "No chance." Then I puff out a sigh. Even with a powerful—though how powerful is yet to be discov-ered—witch on our side, the thought of going up against Axel is terrifying.

Because if he gets through us, who knows who he'll go after next.

"Fine," Skia hisses. *"But please try to be careful."*

"Aww, are you worried?" I ask in a teasing tone. Skia glowers and hops onto my shoulder.

With the kitchen knife clenched tight in my hand, I walk us both into the foyer.

· • ● ● ● • ● ● • •

I meet the others at the front door just as a heavy thud slams against the wood.

"Keep that up," Nona says to Agatha.

My friend has pulled her dark hair into a ponytail and has both hands out, pouring defensive magic into the doorway.

Kate takes the stairs, standing a few steps up with her blade at the ready. Agatha and Nona face the door head-on, and I'm to the right, my breath shallow as what I can only assume is Axel's body or boot hits the door again.

Missy waits under the table beside the stairs. She glances at me for a brief moment before turning her attention back to the door. Her tail swishes silently back and forth.

"One more should do it." Nona raises a walking cane in her left hand, the right fingers twisted and tight as blue electric light sparks across her skin.

My eyes widen. A chest-tightening reminder of the witches who tried to kill me and force Skia back to hell briefly engulfs my focus. I swallow down the memory. Kate, standing across from me on the stairs, looks as awed and frightened as I feel. She stares at her grandmother like she's never seen the woman before.

The one more comes swift and hard. The warped air around the door fractures and dissolves as Agatha lowers her hands.

"You okay?" I shoot her a glance.

She nods, sweat on her brow. "He's strong."

Nona cackles. "Good."

The door splinters and crashes open. Wood flies across the room, shards hitting everyone except Ags, who manages to pop up her shield bubble just in time.

Standing in the doorway, the hulking figure of a hellish Australian bounty hunter blocks the moonlight.

"Well, well, well," Axel says. I assume he looks at each of us, though it's impossible to tell through the thick aviator sunglasses. "Looks like I'm raking in quite the payday."

Kate scowls. "Yeah, I don't think so, dude."

He sneers, turning his head toward the stairs. "You reek of untamed magic. Which means you've cast a spell recently. Hell will pay a lot to find out how you came into witchcraft."

"Hmm." Nona shifts, the cane in her hand directed at the man even as a curious expression flitters across her face. "Why?" She jerks her head in my direction. "I understand the desire to bring back one of their own. It doesn't look good for a shadow demon to be running free when the more powerful forces are still locked away. But why go after spellcasters? Why collect magic items?"

My palms are damp with sweat. The kitchen knife is worn from use, finger grooves not quite fitting to my larger hand.

Axel shrugs. "I don't ask questions when this much gold is on the line."

"Gold?" Agatha raises an eyebrow. Her hands tremble, from the exertion of the protection on the door or fear.

At this, the bounty hunter gestures toward the ground with the weapon in his hand. "They haven't updated to direct deposit down there."

Kate snorts.

"I'm afraid you won't be receiving a payday," Nona says. "Not after attacking these kind children and threatening my granddaughter."

She raises the cane. A blast of light shoots through the room, white-hot and electric. Skia slips down my back, clinging to my waist as they hide from the brightness.

I bring up my hand to protect my eyes, but before I've gotten halfway the light is gone.

A laugh cuts through the air. I swallow, heart pounding as fear cuts in again.

Axel stands in front of the door. Lightly smoking, but otherwise uninjured. He laughs harder, pointing his blade at Nona. "That would have hurt, witch. I'm not a betting man, but I'd put money down on hell payin' more for you than the rest of them put together."

Kate lets out a furious curse, and Agatha steps in front of Nona with her hands raised in a defensive gesture I've seen before.

But my attention is not caught on his words. I frown, head tilted as the bits of smoke coming off his leather jacket seem to follow an invisible trail to the silver charm hooked at his belt.

It glows, ever so faintly. I grit my teeth with realization.

"Impressive protection," Nona murmurs. She doesn't look or sound as confident as she had a moment ago. "A gift from your employers?"

Axel grins. "Something like that. Now, I don't have room for all of you on my bike. But the demon will fit in a cage, and the heart of a witch is worth almost as much as the whole."

He tosses me a secondary glance. "I don't suppose you have a human bounty anywhere? Or are you a complete waste of my time?"

Heat rushes to my cheeks as a combination of embarrassment and fury slams through my veins. I open my mouth to respond.

A high-pitched yowl, amplified to ear-shattering volume by the vaulted ceiling, splits the air.

Missy launches out from under the table, aiming straight for Axel.

Nine

"Missy!" I lunge. Bone-deep worry for my cat overrides any sense of self-preservation.

The little black ball of fluffy feline fury moves quicker than I've ever seen. She swipes. Her claws go through the leather cord holding Axel's silver charm to his belt. The small ball thunks onto the hardwood floor.

Missy bats it across the room and darts to her spot under the table just as Axel's boot flies past where she'd just been.

I'm still moving. Not as quick as my cat, and definitely not as able to stop or turn on a dime.

The realization that Missy is out of an immediate range of harm comes too late. I slam into Axel hard enough to knock him back. He hits the doorframe. Swings his arm.

A burst of pain erupts across my side, and a scream escapes my lips.

Jumbled sounds are just audible past my own heartbeat and heavy breathing.

Agatha shouts my name, high and shrill and more terrified than I've ever heard her before.

Skia hisses the same, rage erupting into all our heads as the little demon screeches bloody murder.

Footsteps pound on the stairs and Kate is at my side, helping lift me from the ground and backing us both away from Axel's blade. The shiny silver is coated in my blood.

The final sound is familiar. Sharp crackling, like a brush fire or dry air right before a thunderstorm.

My vision is blurred, but I make out the fear plastered across Axel's face. He lost his sunglasses while stabbing me.

He meets my gaze for a split second, mouth open as though he's going to try another threat or beg for his life.

He doesn't have time to utter a sound.

I shield my eyes again, and lightning slams into his chest.

With no protection, the scent of burning leather, then flesh, quickly engulfs the room. I look at Nona, hunched over with effort as she goes Emperor Palpatine on the Australian bounty hunter. Her face is red, hair almost glowing with the same blue/white light. But the light begins to fade. The electricity sputters, the line thinning though Axel is still standing.

Agatha is transfixed by the ancient powerful figure Nona is in this moment. My friend glances at me, clenches her jaw, and puts a hand on Nona's arm.

At once, the power amplifies. I have to close my eyes; the light is too bright. I feel a warmth on my chest and recognize Missy's claws as she gently kneads them into my shirt.

And then it's done.

The sound ends. My eyelids no longer glow with the brilliance of the lightning.

I open them slowly, half terrified of what I will see. But where I'd expect a charred corpse is simply a pile of ash and melted metal. The wire frames from Axel's aviators are a few feet away. One of the shades is missing.

"Is..." Agatha's voice is hoarse, as though she's been screaming. "Is everyone okay?"

Kate replies, her voice higher than usual, "Demi needs help."

"Nah, I'm—" I'm about to say fine when a set of kitty toe-beans plant onto my lips. Missy glares at me from her spot on my chest.

Just below her, my shirt is torn and a bloody gash oozes like a babbling brook, staining the wood of the stairs a lovely maroon color.

It occurs to me, as the thought floats across the front of my mind, that blood loss might be affecting my cognition.

"Demi." Skia is at my side in a flash. They curl around the railing of the stairs, eyes narrowed on my wound and then on my hazel eyes. *"What were you thinking?"*

I open my mouth.

"Never mind," Skia growls. *"I know. Missy was in danger. Agatha!"*

She's with us before he finishes saying her name, crouched in front of me—there is no room on the stairs with my sprawling limbs and Kate still behind me cradling my head.

Huh. I try to lift it. I manage to get free of her hands, but the effort makes me dizzy. I lean back again.

"Dammit," Agatha mutters. "Demi, hold still okay? I'm going to try something."

"Maybe some gauze or something?" I ask, my voice slurred.

She shakes her head and plants her hands on my side. I want to protest. She's getting blood all over her lacey sleeves.

But my voice isn't working. My mouth isn't moving properly. The blur moves in, the faces of my family fading as the pain in my side also fades.

I swallow. I wanted to say something. Wanted my final words to be a bit more substantial than "some gauze or something." But I've lost my chance.

It's not fear that grips me now. Now the pain has turned to numbness, I have room for other sensations. Overwhelming warmth fills my chest. I never expected to die this young, but I also never expected to do it surrounded by people who care for me. Who love me.

I feel the smile on my lips, the pressure of Missy on my chest, and the coal-like heat of Skia, their little tendrils twisted around my hand.

And then I don't feel anything.

Ten

Waking up is something like a slow-motion rewind of an old VHS tape. Scenes play out across my eyelids. Axel barging through the door. His charm fending off Nona's power. Missy's daring leap to destroy his protection. My foolish move to try and keep my cat safe.

The knife.

The blood.

I open my eyes, and my vision returns the same way it went, everything fading back into existence.

Agatha kneels on the ground before me. Her hands, sleeves, and skirts are soaked with blood. She's still pressing her hands to my side. Pale fingers are latched around her wrists, and I turn my head just enough to spot Kate looking absolutely exhausted on the step behind me.

"What happened?" I mumble. My mouth is so dry it hurts to talk.

Ags looks up, and my eyes widen at the tear tracks running down her cheeks. "Demi," she breathes.

Missy yowls, rubbing her head across my chin and licking my cheek with her sand-papery tongue.

Skia lets out a hitched sob of relief in my head.

Behind Ags, Nona looks on with a tired gaze. "That was impressive work, Agatha."

My friend moves her hands from my side. The gash across my skin is entirely scabbed over. The sight of it brings back some pain, but nothing like the searing agony that was present a few moments ago.

"Couldn't have done it without Kate," Ags says, giving the woman behind me a grateful nod.

I attempt to sit straight, but everything sways before me. Hands go up, gesturing me to stop moving. "Fine," I say, my mouth still not quite working. "But would someone tell me what happened?"

Skia bobs a bit on the stair railing. "*And maybe we can get them some water?*"

I nod, a poor choice as everything continues bobbing up and down long after my head stops moving.

"Agreed," Nona says softly. "Perhaps we retire to the living room, let Demi lay down for a bit, and refill everyone with some food."

"Sounds great," I groan. "How am I getting there?"

Two days later we are all still at Nona's ranch. Kate called her roommate to reassure her that she wasn't a missing person, and

Agatha did the same with her landlord, blaming the mess on vandals and promising to pay for the windows as soon as she returns.

My apartment was locked when we left so my only concerns are my leftovers going bad and my plants needing a good soak when we get back.

Nona's front door is fixed. Agatha has been pouring over spell books since the morning after my near-death-experience. It didn't take her long to find one to mend simple things, though it did take a few tries to get the entire door back into place without any missing pieces.

I plop another mini-cinnamon roll into my mouth and follow it up with a sip from my nearly black coffee. The little shoebox on the table before me jiggles.

Missy bats at it with a paw but stops when I offer her a strip of bacon.

"*I would like more of the fried pig as well,*" Skia hisses from their place beside me.

At the stove, Kate chuckles and uses a pair of tongs to set three more strips on Skia's plate.

"You're sure you have to leave?" Nona asks, her gaze lovingly fixed on her granddaughter.

Kate nods. "School is starting soon. I need to go talk to my counselor and re-adjust my schedule."

I grin.

We both plan on leaving gaps in our classes so there is time to drive out here every other week or so. Kate and Agatha both have a lot to learn in the magic department and, while I don't have the innate magic they do, I plan on at least reading up on the history of all this stuff.

Nona turns her gaze on me, and her expression grows serious. "Demi, come with me a moment would you? We have something to discuss."

She inclines her head at Missy, who nods and darts from the table after her.

I glance at Skia, who does their bouncy shrug, and then stand with a groan and follow the woman into the living room. The couch cushions are a little stained with my blood, but it's difficult to see unless you're looking for it. The maroon and gold patterned fabric is a good disguise.

"My dear," she says, turning to face me as Missy jumps onto the coffee table before the fireplace. "You already know you don't have any latent magical ability."

My face flushes. I nod, biting away the disappointment that comes with her words.

"However, you do have this cat."

Missy's yellow gaze surveys Nona. I almost imagine she raises a kitty eyebrow.

"Missy is really smart," I say, unsure where this is going.

"Well, she's more than that, actually. She has all the makings of a familiar. And, while it will take a lot more work from you than your friends, with her help you may be able to learn how to practice magic."

My jaw goes slack. I glance at Missy and find her staring at me with a similar stunned expression. Sort of like the time I dropped her tuna treats down the sink on accident.

"She could..." I stumble over the words, looking from Missy to my own hands with excitement trembling in my veins. "We could do magic together?"

Nona shrugs. "It's very possible. This is the most intelligent animal I've ever come across. And she has a connection to the mystical elements of the world. It will take work, mind you." Her eyes narrow into a very school-teacher expression. "Lots of work."

"I don't mind work," I murmur. My skin buzzes with anticipation. I want to start now, to pull down a spell book and train immediately. But logic overrides the idea of staying here another week to get started.

We have time. Lots of time. And Agatha knows a few people who might have some of that latent magic Nona was telling us about. We plan on bringing them next time.

"Now." Nona pats my arm and winks. "We'd better go de-lizard that young man before he develops a permanent taste for grasshoppers."

I snort. The old woman returns to the kitchen, and I crouch with a wince to get even with Missy's eyeline.

"Hey pretty girl." I reach behind her ears and give the scratches she loves so much. "Who knew you'd be so powerful, huh?"

Her nose twitches. She licks me.

Nona waits until the car is packed (she's sending us with copious amounts of gingersnap cookies and magical texts) before she undoes Kate's spell on Trevor.

It takes a surprisingly short amount of time. She mutters a few words, throws a grayish concoction on his lizard body, and then the scales melt away. The lizard is replaced by a tall man with a mop of brown hair and a tank-top tan.

The tan is visible because the poor guy returned to human form without the blessing of clothes.

Kate chucks a spare pair of shorts and a T-shirt at him while the rest of us avert our gazes. Then, Nona steps forward for a few words.

"It's been a rough few days for you. And I'm sorry it took us so long to get you back to two legs. We were all a bit drained for a while there. Now, I know my Kate didn't behave in the most mature way, but I want you to hear me right now."

She moves closer, her finger pressing into the buttons of his borrowed shirt. "You remember those little grasshoppers you ate as a lizard? The crunch of the exoskeleton and the papery texture of the wings? If you do or say anything to put my granddaughter in jeopardy, you will not have the luxury of being turned into a lizard. You will be a bug."

Her tone is kind and old womanly, but her words cause Trevor to blanch.

He nods fervently, glances at the lot of us, then follows Kate's pointed finger to the car waiting out front.

It's a tense drive home. We drop Trevor off at his frat house. Agatha follows him to the porch steps, giving another warning for him to keep his mouth shut—and probably reminding him why he was turned into a lizard to begin with—before letting him go inside.

We stop by the Emporium. I can feel Agatha's sadness at the state of her store, but she puts on a smile and shakes her head. "It's fine." She wiggles her many ringed fingers. "I know how to use magic to fix things."

It doesn't look like much was stolen, but she and Kate work together to at least patch up the glass windows so we can lock the place.

"That will do for now." Agatha heaves a sigh and wipes her brow. Then she looks at me. "Chinese? Your place?"

I grin and turn at Kate. "Wanna join? We know a place with the best egg rolls."

Our new friend smiles but shakes her head. "I really should check in with my roommates. At this point they probably don't believe my texts. I don't want them calling the cops about a missing person."

"Fair enough," I say with a chuckle.

"But I'll give you guys a call tomorrow?" Kate glances between the two of us with slight apprehension. "I'd love to come help fix up the Emporium."

Agatha nods. "We'd love that too."

It's a quiet rest of the evening. The food is delicious. Skia talks me into ordering an extra side of dumplings, and they practically inhale them all before letting them cool. The steam rising up from their shadowy form makes me burst out laughing.

I clutch my side as my scab flares with pain. But it fades quickly. We settle onto the couch. Missy on my lap, eating canned tuna from a pretty porcelain bowl. Skia is in the planters above us, their shadowy tendrils reaching down every now and then to grab an additional spring roll.

Agatha sits beside me, ignoring the Psych rerun and the food in favor of the book she borrowed from Nona. "This is fascinating," she murmurs, her dark eyes scanning the pages with awe.

I dig through my take-out box with my chopsticks, searching for the last piece of broccoli. "It was kind of Nona to share them with us."

She nods, pulled from the book as her gaze meets mine. "It's kind of her to train us, and to open her home to anyone else who wants to learn."

"You're starting something amazing," I say to her, my heart warming with the words.

Agatha shakes her head and reaches over to scratch behind Missy's ears. The cat looks up briefly before deciding scratches aren't interrupting her meal and continues eating.

"Technically," Agatha chuckles, "this one started something amazing."

"*You all did,*" Skia hisses.

"We," I correct immediately. "*We* all did."

"We sure did," Ags says with a smile. "And I can't wait to see where it goes from here."

Thank you

My darling readers... I cannot express my gratitude enough. Spooky Cat started as a fun story with a bunch of bits (like the contact lenses for a cat). It has grown to a whole world with endless possibilities. I plan on continuing to write these little adventures; with magic growing in the world, there is a lot to explore.

www.ingramcontent.com/pod-product-compliance
Lightning Source LLC
Chambersburg PA
CBHW030012010826
48973CB00009B/2779